Night Chillers

Printed in the USA

Published by Black Cover Press

Editor's Choice

Contact the writer, Jim "Etch" Weicherding, directly at

Jwpisces14@aol.com

This book is dedicated to my loving wife Renee and my children, Angela, Valerie, Tanya and Jared.

A special thanks to my daughter Angela for her editing skills.

CHAPTER ONE

'This storm is travelling at speeds of 25 to 35 miles per hour, due north/northeast. It is expected to bring accumulations anywhere from 10 to 18 inches of snow and ice to the New England area before it's said and done, starting around lunchtime today. Commuters can expect travel during rush hour to be a slippery mess. It is highly recommended that you head home earlier rather than later.'

'That's right Gary! New Englanders better stock up on bread and milk today, it's gonna be a long weekend. Remember to check your flashlight batteries and have lots of candles and matches on hand. Power outages are expected for much of the region due to the heavy wet snow and ice. This is gonna be a typical New England Nor'easter.

'Now back to your favorites on Oldies D101.' The deejay's voice is replaced with the song 'Reflections of the Way Life Used to Be'. A hand reaches over and turns up the music on the truck's radio.

"Awesome," Hank mutters. "Shotgun, if your slow ass had been ready when I told you to, we wouldn't have to worry about this stupid storm slowing us down."

"Sorry boss. The old lady was tired. The baby kept her up all night again. I was letting her sleep a couple hours before I left. Shoot me for being a nice guy," his partner responds.

"I just might."

Meanwhile, in a different part of town. "Boss, the truck's all loaded. Can you sign the log and manifest sheet?"

"Yeah. Close up the truck." The boss' voice is tense as he stares out the bay door into the parking lot. "Where are those two idiots? I told them to be here by 6 sharp."

As if on cue, a black pickup truck pulls sideways into the loading area. Two men jump out and the driver smirks as he looks at Shotgun. "We're late, huh?"

"You two clowns get your asses in that truck now. It's already been loaded, since you decided that 6 o'clock really meant eight." He shoves their manifest into Shotgun's hand. "You need to get to Rhode Island and drop off the six containers marked biodegradable to the warehouse for Dr. Seedwick. Then you bring the skids to MedTech and haul your asses back here. No pit stops, ya hear?"

"What's the hurry? This is routine for us," Hank throws at him as he climbs into the driver's seat.

"I've been listening to the weather reports on the band radio frequency and they say there's one hell of a snow storm headed that way and I need Seedwick's shit delivered pronto. You can't be getting stuck in this mess." He shakes his head and goes to walk back into the warehouse before turning back to yell, "You know the deal. Make sure that trailer's temperature is set at 120 degrees or better."

"Yeah, I've been listening to the Rhode Island station too. Why's the trailer gotta be so hot? It's usually 110."

"Just do it! Now get the hell out of here." The door slams behind him.

Shotgun checks the trailer's thermostats before hopping into the passenger's seat of the rig. They read 128 and 125.

"Let's go Hank, I'm freezing to death." While Hank and the boss had been bickering like a couple of school girls, Shotgun had been doing the mandatory inspection of the truck.

Hank reaches for his cassettes while Shotgun puts on the heat and reads over the manifest sheet. The tractor trailer pulls out of the parking lot and rumbles down the road a quarter mile before turning onto the northbound interstate ramp. AC/DC's 'Highway to Hell' plays from the tape deck.

"Breaker 19, Breaker 19, this is Hank the Tank coming at ya. How's the Smokey situation on 95 Northbound? Over."

"Breaker 19, this is Big Rebel coming back from a Maine delivery. I've been rumbling 95 southbound for the last couple of hours and ain't seen a gumball on wheels for a couple of states. Must be preparing for that storm coming this way. Come on back."

"Back at ya Big Rebel. Thanks for the Smokey report. I guess I can put the hammer down and try to beat the storm to New England. This is Hank the Tank and I'm clear. Over."

The driver glares at his partner. "Yo, Shotgun, can you turn the damn heat down? I'm sweating bullets over here."

"Sure Hank." He reaches over to adjust the vents so they blow to his side of the compartment. "Hank, I don't think we're gonna beat this storm to Rhode Island. I've got a bad feeling about the run."

"Don't sweat it Shotgun, I've done this run a dozen times. I could do it in my sleep."

Shotgun looks out his window at the trees and mountains whipping by. "Why do you think we have to keep the trailer so hot, Hank?"

"I dunno, maybe it has something to do with the chemicals we're hauling. Why the sudden interest in the cargo? We've done this run together a half dozen times this year." After a short pause he adds, "I asked you to turn down that heat! It's a freaking sauna in here."

"Alright. Fine!" Shotgun reaches to turn down the heat.

Hank and Shotgun ride for a couple hours, mostly listening to Hank's collection of tapes. The few times Shotgun tries to put anything else on the radio he's immediately ridiculed for his poor taste in 'yuppie crap'. That's about the extent of their conversation. Hank's stressed about beating out the storm and Shotgun's chest and stomach are in knots. He's got a really bad feeling about the trip but he needs this job and can't be acting like a whiny little bitch. It's not like Hank would turn around anyway. He's been driving trucks since he was just a kid out of high school and he's nearing forty now. He's one of the best in the business and he's made it clear to his new partner that if there's a problem with Hank's way, then the new kid can find himself some other place to go. So instead of bringing it up again, Shotgun chain smokes as they fly up the interstate.

"Hey, look. We're making real good time. Maybe we should stop for a quick bite. Between Angie sleeping in and the baby fussing, I didn't get any breakfast." Shotgun needs to get some air and he's not lying about not getting breakfast.

"Yeah, we should grab lunch somewhere. What's it gonna hurt?"

Hank's idea of lunch is a bowl of pretzels and a couple of beers at a strip club he stops at regularly on his runs to northeast states. After a couple beers himself, Shotgun decides to write off the weird vibes he's getting about the run and relax and enjoy the view.

"Hey good looking, come here often?" a dancer asks.

"Nah, I'm just here because Hank, my partner, runs mostly on booze and junk food." He nods towards the driver a couple seats down getting a lap dance. "We're truckers headed north from Virginia." The cute blonde smiles as she takes his ten spot and moves her way down the bar.

A half hour turns into two hours as Shotgun tries to get Hank out of the club. "C'mon Hank, you said a quick bite and we'd be rolling. Let's go!" Shotgun turns to look up at the weather channel on the bar's TV where the anchors are talking about this severe storm tracking further north. While they were hanging out, the snow accumulations had risen higher and the ice threats gotten more dangerous. "Shit, that's all we need! Let's go Hank…NOW!"

While Shotgun is badgering Hank to get rolling, a drunk driver leaving the club backs his car under the trailer. The rear of the car gets hooked on the trailer's heating unit and dislodges a small hose connected to the main compressor. The hose breaks away from the feed panel and the heat vents stop working properly. The thermostat drops down a degree. The drunk driver takes off down the road and drives off the road into the woods.

While this is happening, the truckers are inching their way towards the club's exit to the parking lot. Finally, the doors open and out walk Hank and Shotgun. It's starting to snow and it's even colder than Shotgun remembers. He rubs his hands together before looking at his driver.

"Hank, give me the keys, you've had a little too much to drink."

"I can still drive," Hank slurs with a half-smile on his face.

Shotgun shakes his head. "Give me the keys, you're not driving in that condition."

"You don't know the way." The inebriated driver playfully punches his partner in the shoulder and almost falls over.

"I have a couple thermoses of coffee. You drink the coffee and tell me the way. Deal?"

"I'm not drunk. I just…I just slipped on that there ice." Hank points to the ground where there is no ice.

"I'm not kidding Hank. I've got a kid at home, I'm not getting into the truck with you like this. I, unlike you, have to make it home to take care of my family." Shotgun's getting pissed now.

"Fine. You drive and I'll coffee drink. Crybaby." Hank throws the keys in the general direction of Shotgun then struggles to get into the rig. He almost falls on his ass as he starts laughing. "Ha ha, I said I'll coffee drink. Duh. I meant I'll DRINK COFFEE."

Shotgun walks around the rig doing his safety check and looks at the thermostats. There's only a two degree change but they are still over the manifest temperature requirements. He jumps in the rig, turns the key and off they roll to the song 'Jimmy Mac'.

"Where's the damn coffee? I'm not listening to this dinosaur rock all the way to Rhode Island." Hank takes a sip of the coffee and Shotgun smirks.

"It's hazelnut, do you like it?"

Hank looks over at him. "What do you think?"

Shotgun laughs and turns up the music and heat. The weather is getting worse and Hank isn't getting any better. The coffee hasn't helped sober him up and soon he is passed out in his seat while Shotgun turns the windshield wiper speed up and the music down.

He pulls over at a truck stop right after hitting New York State. 'God, I hope I can remember my way around this New York construction,' he thinks to himself. He looks around and suddenly remembers the route he saw Hank take before. It definitely looks different in the snow. He can hear the cargo shift as he maneuvers his rig around the detour area. "Damn warehouse idiots, don't know how to secure shit."

Shotgun's been driving while Hank snored for some time. Having to actually focus on the road and driving the truck he's only driven a few times has kept his mind off the gnawing feeling in his gut. When he does have a second to notice it's there, he chalks it up to being nervous in the weather. There's a lot of pressure on the both of them to get these deliveries where they need to be within a certain timeframe, and now, since Hank decided to take hours to get out the door of the strip club, they're running behind schedule instead of ahead.

"Finally!" Shotgun shouts as he shifts Hank's truck onto the 95 interstate on-ramp headed north. The big green and white signs read 'New England lanes bear left'. He's through the horrendous construction in New York and as he passes directly under the signs he tells his sleeping coworker, "Soon we'll be in Connecticut. Then it's the Ocean State. We're almost there Buddy. A couple more hours and we'll be offloading. I just hope we don't have to wait out the storm in a motel before we head back." He gets no response. "Yeah, and in that motel room, I'm gonna bend you over and spank you like the bad boy you are." He laughs aloud.

"Huh? Where are we?" Hank sits upright and wipes the drool off the corner of his mouth with the back of his hand. "What'd you just say?"

"I said we're approaching the Connecticut border." Shotgun's still smirking. If Hank had heard what he'd really said, he would have smacked the crap out of him.

"Good." Hank blinks a bunch of times. "The weather don't appear to be letting up."

"You're right, it's gotten a little worse every hour. The damn storm must be to the east of us. I think we're driving into the tail end of the blasted thing."

"Just maintain control of this truck and we should be okay. She's my baby. You hurt her and I hurt you." Hank's only half-joking.

"I'll do my best Hank." Shotgun keeps his eyes on the road and his knuckles are white from how hard he's gripping the steering wheel.

Hank drinks more coffee, which is now ice cold, and watches snow hit the windshield as the wipers flap back and forth, sending snow flying to the edges of the windshield. He sees the 'Welcome to Connecticut' sign.

"See Hank, there's the sign for Connecticut." Shotgun is excited to only be one state away from their destination.

"The roads are getting worse Shotgun. I'll take the wheel in Hartford." Hank's sobered up and is looking over the manifests again. "Find a stop with a Dunkies in the city and I'll grab more coffees and some donuts. You check out the truck while I run inside. It'll only take five minutes."

About an hour later Shotgun finds a T&A with Dunkin' Donuts. Hank runs into the donut shop, brushing snow and sleet off his jacket. He kicks his boots off on the rubber mat then orders two black coffees and a box of plain donuts. As he's paying, a Connecticut state trooper walks in and pushes snow and sleet off his uniform before he tips his hat upside down on the same rubber mat Hank had just used.

"Some storm," Hank says. He's hoping the smell of booze is gone from his breath. He's pretty sure the nasty hazelnut coffee Shotgun gave him was strong enough to cover the smell.

The trooper nods. "Yeah, I'd rather be home in front of a fire with a good Stephen King book." He looks the driver over before putting his hat back on. "Where you headed?"

"North up 95. We've got a delivery that has to be there today." The two stare at each other a minute and Hank gets even more nervous. "So, yeah, everything I've heard indicates this storm isn't gonna end anytime soon. I just heard Rhode Island is almost a total blackout from power outages. You hear anything else? We've been listening to cassettes and there isn't much chatter on the CB."

"I've heard that a lot of roads are impassable. Most of the truckers have found locations to wait out the storm. Maybe you two should do the same." The cop nods at Shotgun, who's doing another parameter check on the truck.

"We do that, we won't have a job when we get home."

"Well, they haven't declared a state of emergency yet so I can't restrict your travel." The trooper shakes his head and walks towards the counter. He turns before placing his order. "Let's just say I'm making a very strong recommendation."

Hank nods. "I appreciate that, I really do. Any other time I'd take that suggestion. But, I've got to get this truck to Rhode Island by 8 o'clock or it's my ass." Hank walks out the door and makes his way to the rig. It isn't until he's back at the truck with Shotgun that he's able to let out the breath he's been holding.

Shotgun has just finished cleaning the hardened snow off the windows of the truck. He's checked the thermostats and they read above the required temperatures so the cargo is still alright. He grabs his coffee from Hank and walks around to get in the passenger's side of the rig. Hank follows suit and throws the box of donuts between the seats.

"What did that cop have to say, Hank?" Shotgun takes a bite out of one of the donuts.

"Nothing much," he lies. He starts the truck and slowly pulls onto the interstate. "Turn on the radio." He wishes at this point that he could heed the trooper's warning. He knows he can't though, especially since the cargo can't get lower than 120 degrees. He stops, and it gets cold, he's fucked. He has learned over the last year that when Boss gives instructions on this particular load, you don't derail from those instructions to save your own life. He'd tried to break off track once and Boss had tracked him down with the truck's GPS. His ass had been smacked right back to the road for delivery. It hadn't mattered that he hadn't slept in over 30 hours. He thought he was a dead man that day, and not for lack of sleep, but because the man that signed his paychecks had murder in his eyes. That was the last time he'd tried to come up with a reason not to get Seedwick's containers to him when he was told to.

Shotgun toys with the radio. "I'm trying to find that Rhode Island station we'd gotten on satellite on the way to the warehouse back home. I don't care what music they play, I just want to be in Rhode Island."

'D101 Providence, your oldies station.'

"You got it Shotgun. That's the one we were listening to."

"Figures." Shotgun mutters as Bobby Darin's 'Dream Lover' starts to play.

Hank manages to muster a smile. "Shut it Kid, I like this song."

The big rig rolls down the highway.

It's not long before they see the 'Welcome to Rhode Island, the Ocean State' sign.

“We’re in Rhode Island, Hank.” Master of the obvious.

“No kidding. Ya think?” Hank rolls his eyes.

Shotgun ignores the older guy’s sarcasm. “Tough to keep this thing on the road isn’t it? It was a bitch back when I was driving it, I can only imagine what it’s like now.”

“Yeah, I’m trying to stay behind that plow about a mile ahead of us but it’s snowing so damn hard I can’t find the groove. Other than a few plows, I think we’re the only idiots on the road.”

“Yeah, I guess.” Again with that feeling in the pit of his stomach. Shotgun snatches the manifest off the dash. “Hey, look for a sign that says ‘Exeter, RI’ and ‘102 north’. That’s our exit.”

“Sure thing.”

‘This special report from the National Weather Service. Be advised that the Nor’easter devastating the New England area over the last several hours has changed course and is expected to head out to sea over the next three to four hours. Stay tuned to this station for detailed reports as more information develops. This has been a message brought to you by the Emergency Broadcast System. D101 Providence.’

Hank lets out a sigh as Righteous Brothers sing ‘You’ve lost that loving feeling’. He’s glad to get some good news for once today. The storm is heading out. At this point he’s wishing he hadn’t answered the phone for this run. If he hadn’t, he wouldn’t be sitting in his rig feeling relieved that some stupid storm is heading out to sea. He plays it off like a pro, but in reality he hates bringing this shit to Seedwick. The dude’s creepy, and the warehouse is locked down tighter than Knox. Sometimes when he’s alone and drunk at night, he’ll start to let his imagination run wild about what goes on in that tiny town in that tiny state and that’s when he falls asleep thanking God that he lives hundreds of miles away. Though sleep after those thoughts is usually followed by nightmares.

CHAPTER TWO

Across town from Seedwick's warehouse, in the home of Mr. and Mrs. Langley, the couple is arguing about what to do in the treacherous weather.

"Darling, we MUST leave. We have no electricity. This means no heat. We'll freeze to death if we stay here," Mrs. Langley pleads with her husband.

"Humph!" the grumpy old man mumbles. "I'm not an idiot, you think I don't know what's going on? The minute we're down the road some punk kid is gonna help himself to everything we have. I am NOT leaving my home, and that's that! Now let it be, Woman."

"Don't be ridiculous Dear, we're only going over to the hospital where everyone else has already gone," she says calmly. Under her breath she mutters, "Even the punk kids."

"No!" He shows no signs of moving from his ratty old recliner where he's reading the newspaper by candlelight.

"Come on Charles, I'll get our coats, you go start the car." She's puttering around the kitchen. "I'll pack us some lunch. It'll be like a picnic."

The elderly man glares at her over the top of his reading glasses. "A picnic? And a hospital full of people? And kids? You know I don't like kids, Liz. Or people. Or picnics for that matter!" He turns the page in the Providence Journal.

Grabbing lunch meats and waters from the fridge, Liz continues to try and reason with her husband. "It's only for a little while. I'm sure the electric company will be by soon to fix whatever the problem may be."

"Fix the problem? FIX the problem? Am I really hearing this? Those fools ARE the problem. They couldn't plug in a toaster without half the town losing power."

Liz is quickly losing patience with her stubborn husband but hides it well. "Now, now Dear. Remember what the doctor said about your temper. It's bad for your heart and your blood pressure." She's packing things into the cooler they keep in the mudroom.

Charles is still sitting in his recliner with his legs up, and bag of chips in his lap and the newspaper wide open. Nastily he retorts, "If he's so worried about my blood pressure, where was he the day before we got married?"

"You know you don't mean that. We've been married for 43 years and I still love you as much as I did when we took our vows." Liz has been dealing with Charles' ill temper since his health began to fail a few years back and what would have once hurt her feelings deeply is now just a jumble of words lashing off her husband's tongue. She can still remember the days when they were happy together.

"Vows written by a woman, no doubt." He starts to cough deeply and grabs his handkerchief, spitting blood into it before grunting and wadding it up to put back into his pocket.

"Charles, you're going to catch your death if you don't get your behind out of that chair right now and come with me to the hospital. Do you really want that?"

"Get off my back Liz. If it'll get you to shut that trap of yours, I'll get up. Jeezus." He pushes the footrest back into his chair and, breathing with great difficulty, hoists himself up. He blows out the candle and walks into the kitchen, nearly tripping over the packed cooler.

After using the bathroom, Mr. Langley puts on his coat, grabs the broom and goes out the side door to their car parked in the driveway. "Figures this blasted storm had to hit us on Super bowl weekend. All my plans shot to hell." He struggles through the snow to get to their Chevy Impala. "Oh well," he mutters. "It'll probably be a blowout anyway. The NFC is always winning the goddamn Super bowl." After sweeping some of the snow off the car, he plops into the driver's seat of their vehicle and puts his key in the ignition. The door is still open and a noise in the eerily quiet night grabs his attention. He turns suddenly.

WHAM! WHAM! The bangs are followed by a deep guttural growl…

Charles Langley doesn't have time to think as he is attacked by hideous creatures, creatures that look like nothing he's ever seen before. It's milliseconds before he is completely covered by monsters tearing into his flesh, ripping muscles from the bone, eating him alive. If he'd only foreseen such an event, perhaps he would have been a bit nicer to Mrs. Charles Langley in their last moments together.

Liz is still in the house, waiting on her husband to come back and tell her the car is warm and it's time for them to go when she hears the ruckus. "Dear, what's all the noise?" She opens the door to investigate and gasps. It's a good thing there's a wall beside her as she loses her balance.

"Oh dear God…what are those things? What are they doing in our car?" The Chillers smell fresh flesh and retreat from the car, leaving nothing more of Charles than a heap of broken bones with small patches of mangled flesh, bodily fluids spewed all over the snow, changing it from a beautiful bluish-white to an ugly red and brown.

The disgustingly contorted beings approach Mrs. Langley slowly, baring their teeth in what appears to be a smile, as she watches in shock from the partially open door. She brings her hand to her face, covering her gaping mouth, and utters "Oh my, I forgot to feed the cat." Snapping back to reality, realizing she's being stalked by the ugliest animals, if that's even what they are, that she's ever seen in her life, the elderly woman slams the door shut.

WHAM! WHAM! They're using all their force to crash through the sturdy mahogany door. Within moments they are successful. Liz tumbles backwards into the corner of the counter, lifting her arms to cover her face. Without a second thought, the Chillers envelop her. The sound of them ripping her to pieces, her bones cracking as they rip her apart, can be heard from just outside the now demolished door.

Liz Langley's unfed cat walks up to the door and sticks its head inside the house before she hisses and takes off into the woods.

While the Langley's are meeting their demise, a couple of miles down the road an emergency crew locates a downed power line with a tree hanging across it as well as three other lines.

"There's our problem, Lou. That transformer's wires are shredded and it needs to be insulated. Whose turn is it to go up top?" A member of the electric company sticks his head out the window of the white National Grid truck.

"Pete, you know it's your turn," Lou replies.

"Can't blame a guy for trying." Pete shrugs as he opens his door and steps onto the ground, his heavy boots crunching in the snow.

"Yeah right." Lou rolls his eyes and remains sitting in his warm, comfy truck with a hot coffee in hand. He sips it lightly and watches in the mirror as his partner walks around to the rear of the truck.

"Hey, at least it stopped snowing," Pete shouts back.

"Maybe so, but it hasn't gotten any warmer." Lou huffs before putting his coffee next to Pete's and pushes the release on his seat belt. He climbs out of the truck and meets his friend at the rear of the truck where he's climbing the ladder to the cherry picker bucket. "I'll push the tree limbs off the lines and reconnect the wires at the transformer."

Pete nods as he secures his harnesses. "It's gonna be a long night."

Once in the air, Pete directs his perch to the tree limbs on the lines. Lou is putting out safety cones, which he believes is a complete waste of time in this weather, seeing there isn't a soul on the road. But, it's standard procedure, company policy, all that blah blah bullshit.

Lou decides to verbalize his annoyance. "Hey Pete, why in the hell do I have to put out these stupid cones? It's not like anybody else is out he---." Silence.

"What's that Lou? I can't hear you from up here." Pete's got the moaning of the motor going as he works on the lines. "Lou?" After a brief pause with no response, Pete continues, "Lou, stop fucking around. You know I hate it when you do this shit. Lou? Where the hell are you?" Pete smirks. "Probably sitting back in the truck where it's warm drinking my damn coffee."

WHAM!

Pete's perch begins to shake back and forth. "What the hell? Lou, dammit, knock it off already! You want me to fall out of this damn thing?"

WHAM!

Again, Pete has to hang on for dear life as the perch vibrates back and forth. "That does it. I'm gonna kick your ass from here to---". He looks down beyond the hydraulic lift from the perch. "What the hell is that?" He squints. Like that's going to change the fact that he sees some deformed animal in the bed of his truck.

Growling, a Chiller starts to climb the lift, digging its claws into the metal. Panicking, Pete glances around frantically to see other animals just like it coming from around the truck and out of the woods. "Dear Mother of God, it's the Devil." He throws some of his tools at it but it just keeps on climbing. The grown man pisses his pants as he looks all around him at the fallen wires and branches.

"Oh God! Help me, PLEASE, help me!" In desperation, Pete hoists himself up and climbs out of the bucket onto the pole, continuously looking back at the advancing Chiller. He makes a bold move and attempts to jump from the pole to a tree, but his boot gets caught on a cable hoop connecting the transformer. He struggles to get free, all the while the Chiller advancing to his perch.

The weight of the Chiller moves the perch toward the pole where Pete is hanging upside down. The metal bucket touches a live transformer wire and the fireworks go off. The jolts of electricity are enough to fry the Chiller like a hot dog caught in a blowtorch. Unfortunately, Pete is also caught in the line of fire. Sparks fly everywhere as Pete and the Chiller fall to the snow-covered ground where they resemble extremely large lumps of charcoal left in the grill. With one Chiller obliterated, the five remaining advance on Pete's smoldering body. Before getting within 10 feet of the body they quickly retreat, leaving him untouched.

Meanwhile, in another neck of the cold and dark woods, a local cop is busy at work.

"Yeah, I'm out here at Old Greenville Road and Snake Hill Road. The whole area is without power. Over." Sergeant Mandel slowly shines his spotlight over the apple orchard and across the street to a farmhouse and not too far from it, a row of townhouses.

"I'll tell you one thing. It sure is one cold night out here," he states as he keys the radio from the police car. He's got his window down, listening for the sound of people. In weather like this, a lot of people tend to try and walk where they need to be since it's safer than driving. He's in a really rural area and he wants to make sure he's got his bases covered before he decides to take off.

"Hey, is there anyone out here?" he yells into the quiet night air.

Crunch, Crunch

Footsteps slowly approach the parked cruiser from behind. The officer seems unaware of any noise coming from beyond his vehicle.

Crunch, Crunch

"Hey, who's there? I'm a cop, I can help you." He puts the radio back in its holder.

No response, just the sound of the snow caving in beneath the feet belonging to the approaching steps. He braces himself on the outside of the driver's side door and reaches his head out the window as far as it will go.

"Hey, I said this is a cop. If you need help, please make a noise, say something, throw something. I can't help you if I don't know where you are!" Still no response.

The voice of the dispatcher breaks the silence in the car, causing Mandel to nearly jump out of his skin. "Can you stop and pick me up a big coffee, regular, and a chocolate glazed donut on your way back to the station. Over."

"Not right now Jo. I'm hearing something but I don't know what it is. I'll get back to you."

The sarge turns on his blues and reds, attempting to get a better look at the area around him. "Ok, this is the last time I'm gonna ask. Who is out there? Are you hurt?" By now he's starting to think it's just a deer or something. They're all over the place out here.

Suddenly the passenger's side door opens and Mandel almost messes his pants. "So much for my floating kidneys," his partner says as he plops his ass down in his seat. "Man, it's freezing out here."

"Christ, did you not hear me calling out to see who was making all that noise?" Mandel is furious.

"Sorry, I had my earmuffs on under my hat, I didn't hear you."

"Well, since you were the one I was hearing, there doesn't seem to be anybody around," Mandel says with a shrug.

"I know. Everybody must be at the hospital. We should take a ride over there and make sure everything's alright." His partner is rubbing his hands together above the heating vents.

"Jo wants us to bring her a coffee and donut," Mandel says as he starts the cruiser and cuts out the flashers.

"Where exactly are we supposed to get it? There's no freaking power."

"Good point." The sergeant gets on the radio and tells his dispatcher she's out of luck, Dunkies can't exactly be serving coffee and donuts with no power.

"Great, now let's get over to that hospital," Officer Young states emphatically once his partner is done on the radio.

"Don't you mean get over to the hospital and make sure that pretty little new RN is alright?" Sergeant Mandel smiles.

"Yeah, I'll see if Jill's okay. What's wrong with that?" The cop sips the coffee he'd made at the station before heading out on the road.

"Have you even asked her out yet, you wuss?"

GROWL

"What was that?" Mandel quickly flashes his spotlight in the direction of the noise.

GROWWWLLLL

He flashes the light far to the right.

Another GROWL

He shines it far to the left.

"What the hell is going on Sarge?" asks Young as he unclips his gun from its holster.

"I don't know, maybe a couple of watch dogs got loose or something." The sergeant's eyes are darting all over the place trying to find the source of the growling, which is now accompanied by the sounds of crunching snow

"I can't see anything," Young states.

Just then, now directly in the line of the shining spotlight, Chillers can be seen advancing towards the officers.

"I don't like this. Call for assistance. NOW!" Mandel goes for his revolver. Young reaches for the radio and keys the mic while Mandel yells into the night, "Identify yourself or I'll be forced to fire." The Chillers continue to come up on the officers in their patrol car. "This is your last warning! Freeze or I'll shoot!" Sgt Mandel blinks his eyes rapidly in disbelief. "What the---?"

BANG! BANG! BANG!

The sergeant pulls his trigger three times, shooting at the hideous creatures picking up speed as they approach. Young can't believe what he's seeing and utters, "It can't be…this can't be happening." The dispatcher back at the station hears everything.

"What is it Roy?" She gets no answer.

"Roy, what's the situation? Roy? ROY!"

More shots are fired as Young quickly gets up and out of the patrol car, gun blazing. Both officers are now standing side by side at the front of the cruiser unloading their guns at the Chillers. They manage to hit some of the advancing beasts but the remaining Chillers tear apart their screaming victims.

All that can be heard on the radio now is static. Jo's still keying and yelling, "Roy, Roy, Respond!"

When they're finished chomping the cops to bits, the Chillers jump into the police car looking for another victim. They hit the switch for flashers and the lights can be seen reflecting off the snow and ice approximately half a mile away where a phone crew has stopped to fix a cracked telephone pole clipped by a fallen tree.

"Hey, look, the cops must be writing some guy over there a ticket for skiing without a license," the smartass foreman says sarcastically.

The other two workers laugh.

"Yeah, funny, huh? I just got a ticket the other day," Rick states. "Rat bastards, got nothing better to do than pull my ass over."

"For what, driving ugly?" Chris punches his boss in the shoulder.

"Ha ha." Rick doesn't think it's funny. He got a $250 ticket for speeding and not wearing his seatbelt. His friends start to crack up.

"Alright, enough kidding around. We need to brace a pole to this cracked one before it splits in two and we have to replace the whole fucking unit."

The three men walk to the trailer containing four half size poles used specifically for supporting cracked units. Chris is still chuckling.

Rick points to one of the logs. "Hoist that one over and we'll lag it to the existing pole. The field manager said a check of this area shows only four splits so we should be home by dawn."

Growl

"Hey, is that your stomach growling? I told you to have something when we stopped for supper."

"I did, I had a salad," Larry, the third guy, states.

"A salad? That's not real food." Rick rolls his eyes. His guys knew they were going to be out all night, why the hell didn't they eat a decent meal before getting on the road.

"I know but my wife thinks I should lose a few pounds. Figures." Larry looks toward Chris.

Chris' head is down as he works on getting the bracing pole loose and he replies mockingly. "It's a miracle she didn't just ask you to cut off your head." He smiles, thinking he's funny shit. Until he turns his head toward Larry and his smile turns to a look of sheer terror as a Chiller rips off his friend's head.

"SHIT!" he yells as he wonders how he's going to escape the same fate as his friend. He backs away from Larry as if in slow motion while the creature spits out Larry's head and moves on to dig into the rest of his body. The thing has one paw, or hand, whatever the fuck it is, on the man's torso like a lion and begins to tear him limb from limb.

Chris can see two more Chillers at the end of the trailer where Rick is and screams. "RICKY!!!! GET OUT OF HERE!" He turns to run through the snow wondering if he'll be able to escape.

"NOOOO!!!" He's screaming as he swings his arms and pumps his legs, running harder than he's ever run in his life, moving further into the darkness. He turns back to look towards the flash of the truck's lights reflecting off the snow and ice. Gasping for air, he bends over to put his hands on his thighs.

"They don't know where I am," he says softly to himself. He watches the four Chillers moving methodically around the truck. "I've got to keep moving," he mumbles, breathing heavy and still gasping for air. He turns away from the truck and makes one step forward when, without any warning, the fifth Chiller snaps its jaws around his legs. It's like a ferret with its death-grip and he quickly goes into shock. The Chiller amputates his legs with its teeth and starts loudly snorting as it devours the tendons and ligaments, ripping his muscle from the bone like a starving kid devours a turkey leg on Thanksgiving day.

Chris' body falls to the snow covered ground in a pool of blood. The others are done consuming Rick and Larry and quickly advance to cover it. Two of the Chillers glance up briefly to look in the distance and see lights before finishing what's left of Chris, leaving behind nothing but shattered bones, just like with their other victims.

The lights they see are coming from the hospital where the town's people have taken refuge until they regain electricity and heat. They know they are safe in the hospital. Or are they?

CHAPTER THREE

"There's our exit, Hank." Shotgun is squinting, it's a little tough to see with the falling snow and absolutely no lights along the highway lit up. "102 North, right up here."

"I see it Shotgun." Hank starts to pump the breaks in the truck, shifting through the lower gears. "We just need to take it slow." He glances quickly at his partner. "What time you got?"

"It's quarter til six," Shotgun replies.

"Good, we should have no problem dropping off Seedwick's parcels by 8:00. We'll drop off the Medtech chemicals on the way back. His warehouse is the furthest away and Medtech has receivers 24 hours a day."

The big rig continues its slow drive north on Route 102 to its first destination, the warehouse of Dr. Seedwick.

The small roads of Rhode Island were not engineered to cater to the needs of eighteen-wheelers and the men ride in silence as Hank does his best to keep his baby on the road. It's difficult to discern where the roads end and the ditches begin. The truck veers more than a few times, but Hank has been driving it for more than two decades and his skill comes in handy in these nasty New England winter conditions.

"Hey Hank, have you noticed anything strange as we're travelling through these small towns?" Shotgun breaks the silence after what feels to him like forever.

"No? What are you talking about, you loon?"

"There are no lights. Anywhere. I don't see any lights in the houses, stores, anything." He's staring out the window with his lips drawn in, more than a bit nervous about their eerily dark and quiet surroundings. That gnawing feeling in his gut has come back with a vengeance and gets worse with every mile they drive.

"Yeah I noticed. It's gotta be because of power outages. We've passed a bunch of downed lines and trees. Everything's covered with snow and ice. That shit's heavy, probably blew out everything for miles." Hank raises his eyebrows. He's always known Shotgun was quirky, but for him to find it odd that there are no lights in a power outage is more than Hank can handle.

“Kinda creepy, don’t you think?” Shotgun whispers like he’s an eight-year-old telling a scary story beside a campfire. “Why aren’t there any candles burning or anything? There’s absolutely NO light anywhere.”

“Dude, what’s wrong with you? It’s only some power outages, not anything to get freaked out about. Wanna call your momma to hold your hand?”

“That’s original.” Shotguns shakes his head and lets out a sigh.

“This is New England, Shotgun. They set up safe shelters for people during storms like these, it’s much worse up here than we could ever imagine down in Virginia. I bet everyone’s all in their high school auditoriums or something because they’re probably not gonna send out crews to fix anything until the storm’s over, or close to it.” He kinda feels bad for the rookie.

“Yeah, I guess you’re right. I just keep getting a bad feeling about this run.”

Hank ignores the passenger’s comment about having a bad feeling. He’d never admit it, but on some level, he’s got a strange feeling too. “This road we’re on brings us right into Chepachet. We take a right onto Route 44 and Dr. Seedwick’s warehouse is gonna be down a nasty dirt road. Keep your eyes peeled for signs showing the way to Cedar Hunt Trail and give me a donut.”

Shotgun reaches for the box. Suddenly the rig swerves back and forth while Hank once again struggles to keep the truck on the road. Shotgun hangs on for dear life.

Hank manages to stop the truck. “Shotgun, go check out the truck and the temperature in the trailer.”

“Here? Right now?” For a brief second he feels his sphincter loosen and he’s afraid he’s going to mess himself. He’s scared to death.

“Dammit, just do it! Quit being such a fucking baby. And where are those damn donuts?”

Shotgun throws on his Red Sox cap and jumps down from the rig. “Why do I always have to do the shit work?” he mumbles to himself. “Jesus it’s freezing out here.” He clears the snow off the thermostats to see there’s been no change. They’re frozen. “ Awesome. At least he can’t bitch at me about this.” He wipes the snow off the lights and reflectors around the truck, glancing around nervously at every sound he hears. While he wipes the snow off the last light he hears something close by walking up behind him. CRUNCH, CRUNCH. Whatever it is, the snow is cracking beneath its weight.

"Oh my God, oh my God," Shotgun whispers quietly. "I'm a dead man, I just know it." He slowly turns his head around. "AAAAHHHHH!!!!" The frightened man screams and slips as he tries to run. "AHHHHH!" Again he screams.

BLAAAARE, BLAAARE!!! The rig's horn blasts. "Will you stop playing with that damn deer and get back in the truck for Christ's sake?" Hank screams out the window.

"Deer?" Shotgun watches as a deer runs down the embankment into the woods. "A deer? I just almost killed myself trying to run from a freaking deer?" Embarrassed, he stands up to wipe the snow off his clothes and jumps back into the truck.

"Your daddy must be real proud," Hank chides as Shotgun slams his door shut. "His offspring having a heart attack over his fear of Bambi. Hahahaha." Hank laughs as he starts the truck. "I hope we don't run into Thumper at our next stop."

Lightly chuckling himself, Shotgun looks out the window and whispers, "That thing scared the shit out of me." His heartbeat starts to slow down as he takes deep, intentional breaths.

A few miles up the road Shotgun spots where they're supposed to turn. "Hank, there's Route 44, we take a right and head east." He takes a sip of his now-cold coffee. "Yeah Boy, we're almost there."

Out of nowhere Hank mumbles to himself, "What the hell does Chepachet stand for?" He turns the rig slowly onto Route 44 and heads east.

About a half hour later the men turn off the main road onto a back road that leads to the warehouse owned by Dr. Seedwick.

"I still haven't seen any lights Hank," Shotgun states.

"I know, I know, me neither." He nods ahead of them. "There's the warehouse, let's hope somebody is still here." Hank's holding his breath as he pulls the truck around back to the loading platform and backs it in. "Shotgun, make sure this clown signs the manifest papers and puts we made it before 8:00pm." Hank looks down at his watch. "It's 7:45pm."

"Aren't you coming with me?" Shotgun almost whimpers.

"Why, you afraid you're gonna run into Bambi again?" Hanks snickers.

"No. I don't know where to get thesc parcels delivered to inside." He points to the building. "In case you haven't noticed, this is a big place."

"Alright, fine, we'll both go. I have to hang ten anyway."

They guys walk sided by side up the steps to the back door and ring the buzzer.

"I didn't hear the buzzer, did you?" Hank asks his partner.

"No. I'll try again." Shotgun pushes the button again. They wait a minute or so and get no response. "Now what're we gonna do now Hank?"

"I'll go around front and see if somebody is in the office area." Hank jumps down to the parking lot. "Not that anyone's gonna be there," he mumbles as he walks off through the snow.

"Hank, wait!"

"Don't worry kid, I'll be right back."

Shotgun stands shivering, looking around the moonlit parking lot to the beginning of the woods. The snow is tapering off and the full moon lights up the sky. "C'mon Hank, where are you?" He puts his hand on the doorknob and waits.

RAAAGGGHHH!!!

Hank suddenly jumps out from just beyond the corner of the warehouse wall. Shotgun jumps, inadvertently turns the knob and falls inside the entrance to the building.

Hank runs up the steps. "Wouldn't you know it, the damn door was unlocked the whole time." He helps Shotgun to his feet. Once inside, Hank flips the light switches a couple times. "Kid, go grab the flashlight out of the truck. None of the lights are coming on."

Shotgun runs as fast as he can to the truck and gets the flashlights before running back into the warehouse. He's so scattered he almost knocks Hank over as he rushes back through the door. He has that same feeling creeping up the back of his neck that he did when he was a kid needing to pee in the middle of the night and jumped out of bed, trying to get away before the boogie man grabbed his feet when they hit the floor.

"Whoa Buddy, slow down. This ain't no fire." Hank takes one of the flashlights and tells Shotgun to stay close. He stops suddenly and Shotgun is all over him.

"Not that close Boy, give me some breathing room. Damn."

"Hank, I'm freezing. It's like a refrigerator in here. Let's just bring in the containers and get the hell out of this place."

"Sorry Man, but I'm not going anywhere without a signature. Now be quiet, you're giving me a headache." They continue to slowly make their way through the warehouse, Hank leading the way.

A few minutes later, out of the blue they hear a Clang, followed by a Bang then a Thud. Hank quickly turns the flashlight toward where the noises are coming from.

"What was that?" whispers Shotgun.

"Shush. I dunno but it came from over there." Hank flicks his wrist, indicating the area from which the noises emerged.

"Can we leave now? I can't feel my toes." Shotgun's heart is beating a million miles a minute and he feels like he's going to throw up. He's scared shitless and just wants to bail. At this point, new kid at home or not, he could care less if he loses his job over this run.

"Not yet. Somebody is in here and I want to find out who it is." Shotgun huffs in disgust and they slowly make their way over to the corner of the warehouse. They still haven't found anyone in the building, but they do find six containers resembling the ones in their trailer broken into big pieces. Hank flashes his light into one of the containers and gradually moves his head closer to the top of its broken shell.

Clang! Bang! Thud. Hank perks up quickly and points to the other side of the warehouse. "Kid, go see what that was," he whispers.

"You're the one with the flashlight." Shotgun glances in the direction of the noises, his eyes wide with fear.

"The moonlight is bright enough in here. You won't walk into a damn wall."

"I think I'll just stay with you."

"Fine! Wait til I tell the guys about this when we get home tomorrow." Hank flashes the light into the damaged container. "What the fuck is that?"

"What is it Hank?"

"Shit if I know. It's some kind of ooze crap." Hank reaches into the container.

"What the hell are you doing Hank? You don't know what that stuff is." Shotgun backs up a few steps, watching his partner in awe.

Hank pulls out a glob of the putrid jelly-like substance. "Look at this shit. Have you ever seen anything like this in your life?" Playing around, he pushes his hand closer to Shotgun, who backs up even further.

"Yeah, in my kid's diaper." It takes all he's got not to puke; the ooze smells even worse than anything he's ever found in his baby's pants. "Let's get the fuck out of here, Hank. I'm not playing games here. Let's GO!"

"Wait! There's a label." Hank shines the light onto the sticker and reads aloud. "**Human and Animal DNA. Keep samples separate. Keep at a temperature of over 100 degrees. Future cloning testing required.** Wow, that's some deep shit."

"Are you seriously telling me this stuff is for cloning? And this is human DNA?" Shotgun is now beyond freaked out. What the hell have they been driving with in the back of their truck?

"It's also animal DNA. Don't forget that part, ha." Hank's sense of humor astounds his partner sometimes.

"Whatever, you sick freak." Shotgun peers into what's left of the container with the goo. "Where in the hell is the rest of this shit? From the looks of it, these containers hold close to twenty gallons of fluids, or whatever the hell that shit is considered, and I only see traces of it left."

"I don't know. But I think you're right. We should probably get the hell out of here." For once, Hank is in agreement with the guy he's spent the last twelve hours hassling.

Crash! Bang! Thud.

GROWL

Hank turns hurriedly and flashes the light back toward the same location as just a few minutes earlier.

Bang! Thud!

GROWLLLL

This time the noise comes from a different location and he flashes his light across to the far corner of the warehouse.

"What was that, Hank? It didn't sound good, at all!" Shotgun's now holding onto the back of Hank's jacket like a scared little kid.

"I dunno Kid, but it's not an 'it'.. it's a, a, uh, I think it's a 'they'…" There is fear in Hank's voice now.

"Ohmigod," Shotgun whispers. He looks around as though he'll be able to see anything in this dark-ass warehouse. "What are we gonna do now?"

"Maybe it's just a couple of cats or something," Hank says, not very convincingly.

GROWWWLLLL

"I ain't ever heard a cat sound like that. So I'll tell you what we're gonna do. We're gonna get the hell out of here." Shotgun pulls on Hank's jacket. "Dude, let's go, no playin', let's get the fuck out of here now."

Hank is curious now, and ignores the annoyance at his back. The flashlight batteries start going dead. "Damn thing." Hank hits the flashlight a couple times. "Figures."

"I saw this happen on a scary movie before, Hank."

"This ain't no movie Kid. Can you see the way we came in at the other end of the warehouse?" Hank decides it's really time to get a move on, curious or not. He knows that something's going on in this building and he's sure he doesn't want to stick around to find out what it is.

"Barely."

"Well, when I tell you, you run like the Devil's on your ass and he's had a bad day. Am I clear?"

"Crystal," Shotgun mumbles under his breath.

"On the count of three we take off. Got it?" Hank shakes his buddy's hand and tells him not to stop for anything until they make it to the truck.

"Okay, here we go....THREE!" Hank yells.

"Three?" Shotgun yells as they both start to run side by side through the dimly lit warehouse.

Slam! Crash! Bang!

Noises erupt all around them as they reach the point halfway between the containers and the door. "Keep running Kid!" Hank yells to Shotgun.

The sounds echo everywhere as Shotgun pulls open the exit door with Hank one step behind. He emerges out the door out of breath as it swings back shut with a thud.

Hank grunts as he pulls the exit door open and yells, "Run Kid, run! We're almost there!!!"

CHAPTER FOUR

"Well?" Al's mom asks the nurse on duty impatiently. She's wringing her hands nervously.

"Your son has a temperature of 103, most likely caused by the ear infection. We'll give him a dose of Tylenol along with Motrin and some antibiotics for the infection." Al's mom looks at the nurse with her eyebrows raised. Jill reassures her that her son will be fine. "Because they are different drugs, we can administer both Tylenol and Motrin at the same time for high fevers like this. It's actually common practice to bring down temperatures. Once we've given him the medications we'll put him in a private room for the night so he can rest." The nurse smiles and puts her hand on the woman's shoulder. "He's going to be okay."

"Excuse me, Jill?" Another nurse walks into the examination room. "We have a lot of people in the ER that should be moved to another floor." She smiles at Al and his mother.

"Excuse me just a second," Jill says to her patient. She steps into the hallway with her colleague.

"Okay, let me just finish up here and I'll be along to help." She pauses briefly. "Is it just me, or is it getting cold in here?" asks Jill as she rubs her hands together.

"Nah, it's your imagination. Get some skin on your bones and you won't be so cold," says the other RN.

Jill looks outside and walks over to the window where she thinks she sees shadows move across the snow covered ground. She hears snow crunching under footsteps and quickly looks in their direction. She leans over the heater vent and puts her hand on the window and slowly looks from left to right. Seeing nothing else she shrugs her shoulders and turns to walk back towards the door to the hall.

Outside the window, the Chillers move under the window and go around the corner of the building. Jill again hears something and stops at the door, turning to look back out the window. She has a look of fear on her face, but exits the room and starts down the hall to the ER.

When she gets there she approaches the crowd of people sitting around talking, reading and listening to music. Some of them are even on laptops. "Hey everybody, how about we go downstairs to the cafeteria where we can all grab a bite. Sound good?" she asks, trying to be chipper and upbeat.

Mostly everyone wants to leave. However, a little girl insists she wants to stay put. "The boogie monsters are down there," she says. Jill bends down in front of her and puts her hands on her knees. The little girl, sitting in an ER waiting seat, turns away. "I don't want anything to eat. Give it to the boogie monsters."

"What's your name Sweetie?" asks Jill, trying to get the girl to make eye contact.

"Sarah," the child replies softly.

"That's a nice name. My name is Jill." The nurse smiles. "Where's your mommy, Sarah?"

"She went down there." She points down a hallway that leads to a darkened wing.

"When, Sarah? When did your mommy go down there?"

"A few minutes ago. Before the boogie monsters did." The girl has her arms wrapped around her waist and her blue eyes are wide with fear and sadness.

Another RN overhears the conversation and walks up to Jill. "We took everybody out of that section and shut it down. We only have the hall bulbs on because the generators can only handle heating certain areas of the hospital. God only knows how long we'll even have heat in this section." The woman turns to Sarah. "Did your mommy say where she was going?

"She said she was gonna find the bathroom." The girl refuses to look at this nurse, as she did Jill a moment before.

"Ann, can you take Sarah to the cafeteria? I'll catch up in a few minutes." Jill takes Sarah's hand in her own. "This is Ann, Sarah. I need you to please go with her. She will watch over you until I find your mommy, okay?" The little girl shakes her head. "I know you're scared honey, but I want you to stay with everyone else so you stay warm and safe. I'll be back before you know it!"

"OK," Sarah responds reluctantly. "Jill, look out of the boogie monsters." Jill and Ann just look at each other and smile.

Ann takes Sarah towards the cafeteria. Sarah turns and waves to Jill. Jill waves back before walking around the dark corner in the direction Sarah pointed.

"Hello, is there anybody down here?" yells Jill. No response. She continues slowly down the dark hallway dimly lit by backup lights. "Hello? Sarah's Mom?" Nothing. Jill wonders why she didn't ask Sarah what her mom's name is. "Ma'am, we should get back with everyone else on the other side of the hospital." Silence. "Is anybody down here?" To herself she whispers, "It's freezing down here." She reaches the ladies restroom and pokes her head in. "Sarah's mom?" Again no response. Unbeknownst to Jill, she has been walking in a stream of fresh blood on the hallway floor. She just looks further down the dark hallway.

A faint "Grrr" can be heard. "Who's there? Sarah's mom, is that you?" She waits a moment. "I'm an RN here and your daughter is in the other part of the hospital." She talks to the darkness. Grasping at straws as to why the woman won't respond, she draws her own conclusions about what she's doing. "I won't say anything if you're smoking." She adds under her breath, "even though it's against hospital policy."

GRRRR

"Fine, finish your cigarette. Your daughter can be found with the others. I'm freezing. I'm heading back now. We hope to see you soon." Again, under her breath, she adds, "Nice talking with you." Then she thinks, 'doesn't she know smoking is bad for her health?' What Jill doesn't know is that the Chillers are eagerly devouring Sarah's mom in the dark. She actually had been going for a cigarette, and it's now lying on the ground, the head slowly burning its way toward the filter.

Jill heads back towards the lights and the heat on the other side of the hospital. She gets to the receptionist area and asks if a woman walked out before she did.

"Nope. Haven't seen a soul," the woman behind the desk responds without looking up from her magazine.

Jill walks into the waiting room. Empty. "Everybody must be in the cafeteria," she says aloud. She gets a cold chill and feels her forehead. "I'm not feeling very well." She finds a thermometer and takes her temperature. "Just what I thought. I have a fever. Of a hundred and three of all things." As she disinfects the thermometer she stares out the window at the moonlit snow and ice covering everything.

BANG!

Jill jumps and spills the thermometer holder onto the floor. The sound of shattering glass echoes when the container breaks.

SMASH! CRASH!

The window before her seems to explode. Jill starts screaming, frozen in place. Gaining her composure, she slowly walks over to the dark object lying on the window sill, cautiously reaching out to see who, or what it is.

It jumps up screaming. "They got Hank! They got Hank!" It's Shotgun.

"Oh my God." Jill nearly jumps out of her skin. It's all she can do not to scream.

Shotgun sits there with a glazed look in his eye. He's in shock and Jill tries to get him to calm down.

"Bodies! Everywhere! Torn to shreds. They're all dead. They got Hank. They got Hank. You've got to help me. They got Hank." Shotgun is seemingly in need of mental health attention as he pleads with Jill. He's trembling in fear.

An orderly and another RN run into the room.

"We heard a loud crash come from in here. Are you alright Jill?" the nurse asks.

"Yeah, I'm fine. We need a gurney. STAT! This man's in shock." She's taking his blood pressure, temperature, pulse ox, all the things that a nurse does whenever anyone comes into the ER, even if it is via the window.

Soon Shotgun is being rolled into an isolation ward where they begin to treat him for shock. They elevate his legs to increase blood flow to his organs and brain. The bluish tint to his skin immediately begins to dissipate and his heart rate begins to decrease. Once his vitals are a bit more stable, they cut his clothing off and wrap him in several blankets. Because of the blackout, they have no access to heated blankets but his body responds to their treatment.

"He's stabilized now," an orderly says to Jill when she comes back into the room after scouting the area for a room into which they can place him. "He's sedated to help him rest. What do you think he was rambling about? Everybody's dead? Hell, more than half the town is in here. And who the hell is Hank?" asks the orderly.

"I don't know, but one thing's for sure. That guy was scared to death of somebody," says Jill.

"Or something," says the other RN. Her hands are clasped together as if she's praying.

The three of them look out the window into the surrounding woods. They then look at each other. Suddenly they're engulfed in darkness.

"What the hell?" asks George, the orderly who's been assisting with Shotgun.

"Another generator just died," Jill sighs. "That means now only half the hospital will have heat and electricity." The backup spotlights come on casting a dim light over the room.

"Great, even our backups are strained. We better get our new visitor to the other part of the hospital," George tells the two nurses.

"Yeah, it'll get cold in here soon, and he needs to stay as warm as possible." Jill is getting frustrated. She mutters, "The damn heaters are stuck on freaking a hundred degrees when they do work and it falls to freezing in ten minutes when they go down. I hope the electric crews get us up and running real soon. We're running out of hospital. You'd think we'd be a priority."

"Let's go already," says the other RN.

Within minutes they've all joined the others on the opposite side of the building. As Jill checks on the residents and patients she begins to freak out.

"Mrs. Brown? Mrs. Brown? Al?" Jill picks up her pace.

"What's your hurry, Girlfriend?" kids George.

"I don't know, but let's hurry." She's got a gnawing feeling in her gut. They start to run toward the dark side of the hospital. It's not long before they hear the mother of Jill's patient that she'd forgotten to move in the chaos of Shotgun's arrival. They've been in the dark for a few minutes now.

"Hello, is anybody here?" Mrs. Brown walks slowly through the dark hallways carrying her ill son. "Hello, we're lost." Her voice is shaky as she tries to find her way through the hospital.

Jill runs alongside the orderly and other RN. "Al and his mom are still over there. We have to go get them."

They start back toward Al's hospital room. "I'm getting so cold." The little boy whimpers. "Mommy, I'm scared."

"It's okay Al, we'll find the others." She rubs her son's head in an attempt to reassure him they're going to be alright.

Al is watching behind his mom as she walks down the hallway. "Mommy, something's behind us."

"Now Allen, honey, this is no time for your imagination to run wild. I know it's scary because it's dark, but there's nothing there sweetheart."

"But Mommy, can't you hear them?" He's shivering in her arms, a culmination of the fever and fear.

A look of fear covers her face as she hears a rustling behind them. "No Al, I don't hear anything," she lies.

"Mommy, I'm scared," the boy reiterates.

"Shh, Al, I see a light up ahead. Maybe that's where everyone is." She picks up her pace.

GRRR…Growl

BANG! A bed pan hits the floor. Mrs. Brown screams and starts a slow jog.

Just then Jill rounds the corner and stands screaming. "Run Mrs. Brown! Run toward me! Run like hell, NOW!"

The woman holds her son as tightly as she can and starts to run out of the darkness. The Chillers are closing in on her and Al. Jill runs and gets a gurney, pushing it as hard as she can past Mrs. Brown and Al into the darkness, blocking the path of the monsters.

Another BANG! Then growls so loud Allen has to cover his ears, as does Jill.

"We can see you Mrs. Brown. Keep running!" Jill screams. Jill runs toward them.

"I can see them! Ohmigod I can see them." Jill screams as she reaches Mrs. Brown and wraps her arms around the mother and her boy. The Chillers begin to cover them, jumping up onto the two women and the boy, knocking them onto the ground. The orderly and second RN turn and run screaming toward the fully lit corridor beyond the darkness. Suddenly the Chillers retreat into the darkness, squealing. The air falls quiet, eerily quiet.

Jill and Mrs. Brown look at each other. "What happened? Are we dead?" Mrs. Brown asks, bewildered.

"Where are those things?" Jill stands up and brushes off her scrubs.

"I don't know but I'm not sticking around to see if they come back." Mrs. Brown grabs her son off the floor and hugs him tighter than she's ever done before.

The three of them walk around the corner into the light.

"Are you okay?" Jill asks Mrs. Brown quietly as she brushes a piece of hair off of Al's face. He's almost catatonic, seemingly unaware of what has just taken place.

"We're alive, that's about as close to okay as I feel right now." She stops and puts her son down on a table in the hallway. "Al, are you okay?" The unresponsive boy's mother looks him over for injuries before covering him in hugs and kisses.

The smothering bout of affection brings him back to reality. "I'm still cold Mommy, I don't feel good." Mrs. Brown laughs nervously, glad that he's talking to her.

Jill feels his forehead.

“Our temperatures.” Jill thinks aloud. “We’re alive because we have fevers.” She looks back into the darkness. “Whatever those things are, they can’t take the heat,” she thinks aloud. “Well, I’m no Zena, and I’m not going back down there. Let’s go get some help.”

The women walk slowly toward the others with growls of anger behind them.

CHAPTER FIVE

"What the hell is that noise?" There's a horrific sound vibrating through the heating ducts and one of the doctors from the second floor looks up at a heating duct.

"Must be one of your patients reading his medical bill," retorts another doctor.

The first just smirks. Just then the orderly and RN run into the cafeteria.

"They killed Jill!"

Everyone looks in their direction.

A second later Jill and Mrs. Brown, carrying Al, walk through the door.

"Ohmigod Jill, we thought you were dead."

"So did I," states the nurse.

Jill fails to hesitate and proceeds to stand on top of a table and start talking loudly. "I want your attention. Everyone. Please listen to me and DO NOT panic. There's something in the hospital. There's more than one of them and I have no clue what they are nor where they came from. I do know one thing about them though. They do not like heat. As long as have power in this section of the hospital we should be safe."

Jill quickly glances at the lights.

"Why did you do that?" asks the orderly, confused.

"Because if this were a movie that would have been the perfect time for the generator to go dead."

"Well, this isn't a movie and apparently we're in trouble. What is here? Where are they now? How do we keep them out of here?" a loud voice from the crowd asks.

"Where in the hospital are they?" Another nervous voice.

"Where are the police?" demands yet another member of the group.

The collection of townspeople has begun to panic and start throwing questions at Jill.

"What do you mean you don't know what they are?" asks one woman in a small voice. Only Jill can hear her because she's directly in front of the table where the nurse stands.

"Can't we just leave the hospital?"

"NO! We cannot leave the hospital. Did you not hear me? They don't like the heat. This probably means they like the cold, don't you think? And in case you all haven't noticed, it's the damn arctic outside." She turns to the woman in front of her. "And I mean, I don't know what the hell they are. " Jill feels her patience slipping and decides she needs to regroup. She sits cross legged on the table and closes her eyes, breathing deeply for a few moments until she feels a calm feeling and once again feels confident she can answer their questions and make them feel a little more at ease.

Once again on her feet, in a calmer tone, Jill once again addresses the crowd. "It's freezing outside everybody. If we leave we'll be walking frozen dinners before we reach the woods. They definitely appear to like the cold. We wouldn't stand a chance out there in the elements."

"But our cars are in the parking lot, I say we make a run for it," says one large man.

"No!" Jill and the orderly yell at the same time.

"Look, I'm not sitting here waiting like this is a catered event and I'm part of the buffet," the man says as he stands. "I'm going."

"No, please, Roy, don't be foolish." A woman pleads.

"I'm not staying either. My truck is only twenty yards away from that door." Another man points toward the exit to the hospital, which can be seen from the cafeteria. "And if Roy over there can make it to his car, then I can make it to my truck."

"C'mon Jim, be reasonable," the guy sitting next to him states. He looks at his buddy like he's being a complete moron.

"You can't make us stay here," another member of the community pipes in.

"No, I can't. I just wish you would," Jill tells everyone.

"C'mon Roy, let's get the hell outta here," Jim states emphatically as he stands.

Roy and Jim walk to the entryway to the cafeteria. "Roy, have your keys ready before we take off," his buddy tells him.

"Alright Jim. I have my keys out. Who's gonna go first?" Roy is a goofy-looking bald guy with the look of innocence always in his eye.

"You are!" Jim pushes Roy out the door. He falls to the ground and quickly gets up. He spots his car across the yard, up in the lot area. He slowly creeps to the end of the building corner. Everything seems to be clear.

"Jim, what the hell did you do that for?" Jill yells. "He's your friend."

"You'll see why in a minute." Jim looks out the door while the others watch out the windows. They see Roy start to run across the snow covered ground.

Roy makes it to the parking lot and slows down, seemingly more sure he's in the clear. Suddenly the Chillers run across the yard after Roy.

Everyone starts screaming, "Run Roy, Run!!! They're right behind you!"

Jim glances at Jill who is glaring at him with fury in her eyes. "He was a good guy. When we were boys we used to call him 'Decoy Roy'. Later." Jim waves and exits the building.

Jill doesn't know what to say as Jim heads toward his truck watching with a sideways glance as the Chillers swarm over Roy's body. "Thanks Roy, I owe ya." He unlocks the door and jumps into his oversized 4x4 and fires it up. He cranks the heat levers to high.

Vroom Vroom…he revs the truck's engine as his loud exhaust roars into the night air.

The Chillers take off after Jim's truck. He wishes he had been able to find a way to get to his truck without sacrificing his lifelong friend, but he knows that the end will be worth the means. He floors the gas pedal and sends snow flying everywhere as he heads for the road, pushing two parked cars into each other, pinning a Chiller screaming amongst the wreckage.

Everybody in the hospital is watching and yelling "Alright Jimmy, kill those damn things!"

Jim's truck backs away from the smashed cars and the dead Chiller falls limply to the ground. He turns around, his right arm slapping the top of the bench seat excitedly as he continues to move backwards.

"Come on you fucking low life monsters. You want to have to catch me?" He looks out of his sliding back window.

Jim's truck goes right by the hospital's windows in reverse so close they could've touched it.

"C'mon James, get 'em!"

Everybody's cheering. For the first time in what seems like forever, they have hope. It's been deduced that there are five of these nasty creatures, and their fellow town member, and friend, just killed one of them. If he keeps up the way he's going, which is likely to happen since he is probably the most determined bastard in town, these things will be gone in no time.

"Kill 'em Jimmy!"

"Run them over!"

The Chillers suddenly run past the windows. There's a different kind of screaming now! Excitement is quickly replaced with heart-in-the-throat fear.

Jim's truck can still be heard roaring in the distance. It then becomes quiet. Everyone stands silently, most of them holding hands, afraid to breathe.

They're disappointed, and scared as shit. They'd thought Jim had gone into the parking lot to help, to rid the town of these grotesque creatures. But they all now realize he had only killed that one Chiller because it got in his way. His intent the whole time, from pushing 'Decoy Roy' out the door to become snack food to smashing the monster between the cars, was just to escape and leave the rest of them hanging.

ROOOARRRR!!!!

Suddenly Jim's truck goes racing forward past the windows. There are Chillers on the roof, the hood and in the bed. Most everyone begins to cheer again; they have a new hero.

The truck is spinning and sliding on the snow and ice in the parking lot. In the cab of the truck the driver quickly jacks the steering wheel left then right, desperately trying to eject the monsters. He watches as they cling to his baby and attempt to advance toward the cab area where he sits. No matter how much he jack-knives the truck, or how many donuts he pulls, these goddamn things will NOT let go. He's sitting behind the wheel of this monstrous vehicle cussing like a sailor.

Suddenly, the truck dies. The battery cable has ripped off the post from bouncing around like a matchbox car on a trampoline. The winter terrain has not been of any assistance either.

Everybody gasps!

"He won't have heat!" The first thing that comes to Jill's mind is that within moments, Jim's truck is going to cool down and there will be nothing keeping the Chillers away.

"They will get him!" an elderly woman screams.

"What are we gonna do?" Everyone is looking around at each other, some with wide eyes, some with tears.

"What are they gonna do to him?" It's Sarah, who still doesn't know that her mother is laying a couple of corridors away, yet another victim to the creatures about to attack Jim.

Jim turns the key frantically in the ignition. "SHIT!" He yells, hitting his hands on the steering wheel. He reaches over and grabs his shotgun off the internal gun rack and opens the drawer. "Goddamn, it's just got three shells. I shouldn't have gone hunting with Roy last Sunday."

The Chillers are desperately waiting to get to Jim. Once the heat in the truck goes away he's done for.

"Maybe not," says Jill to herself. She realizes she's spoken aloud and clarifies. "Maybe not, as in, maybe he's not going to die." She continues, "Let me know when they get close to him." They're all watching him check his rifle.

"Why?" as George, the orderly.

"Just do it!" She has no time for questions or insubordination.

"Now Jill! One's trying to get in through his sliding back window!" the RN that was with her and George in the hallway calls out.

Jill swings open the door and yells. "Hey shitheads! Why would you want a snack when there's an entire meal over here?"

It takes a minute, but a few more people step out into the cold air with Jill. They're catching on to her plan.

The Chillers hear her and take off for the door to the hospital.

"Jim, when I tell you, run for it!" Jill yells.

He climbs out of his truck tentatively. "Now Jill?"

"Not yet, not yet…NOW!" The Chillers are getting closer to the building.

Jill and the others leap back into the hospital and Jill slams the door shut. The Chillers scream in anger and jump at the glass doors. This sends everyone back a few feet, gasping. They expect the monsters to smash through the glass, but realize it's tempered and even if they got in, they wouldn't last a minute in the warmth.

Angrily, the Chillers turn and see that Jimmy has left the safety of his truck. They slowly and methodically advance toward him and his red truck. Jim's quickly loading his rifle.

"C'mon you ugly fucks, you wanna play? I'm not going without a fight!"

The monsters draw nearer. The people in the hospital slowly move toward the windows. Jill has to yell at them to back off a bit, their breath is fogging up the glass.

"GAH!" The entire crowd screams in unison as a Chiller jumps from under the window and startles them.

"They must be pissed for being tricked. Boy these things are intelligent." Jill says. Everybody watches in horror.

BLAM! BLAM!

Jim fires at the Chillers, missing one but wounding another.

"You can kiss my---AAAAAHHHH!!!" Jim screams as he pulls the trigger and the last shell rips through one Chiller's head, sending the creature flying to the ground. It squirms a minute before its lifeless bodies is enveloped in blood-soaked snow.

Jill watches in horror as she brings her hands up to cover her face. "Oh God, Jim's dead." She's fighting back tears.

"Jimmy killed two of those things, Jill. How do we get out when there are still three left?" George's question pulls her back into the moment.

"I don't know. Maybe our power will come back on soon." She looks out the window at Jim's truck. "I just don't know."

Suddenly the lights flicker off then back on again. Jill looks up at the lights, and then down to the faces of the trapped people. They've mostly gone pale, petrified. Many of them holding each other for comfort.

"Jill, I don't think the generator is gonna last much longer under this load," says the maintenance man. He and his assistant slowly approach Jill and the orderly. They've been in the back office of the cafeteria, trying to configure numbers and determine the generator situation.

"Charles, please tell me there's another way out of this hospital?"

"No can do, Jill," he replies.

CHAPTER SIX

Feeling defeated, the nurse sits on top of a table. Tears begin streaming down her cheeks. She feels like she's failed. She feels responsible for the lives of the people in her building.

"What about the corridor in the outpatient clinic building?" Ask Charles' assistant, Zane.

"She wants a way out, not a way to stay in," replies his boss. He rolls his eyes before exclaiming, "Wait a minute! There's an underground hallway to the clinic!"

"Yeah, that's what I was talking about!"

"But it's on the other side of the hospital. Half these people won't make it. Besides, we don't even know if the clinic has any power." Jill jumps up, excited but leery at the same time.

"Somebody has to go find out," George chimes in.

"The clinic has its own generator and must be started manually. It's located beneath the building." Charles leans with his back against the wall, his arms crossed, his utility belt hanging from his waist.

"Is the startup for the generator near the underground access corridor?" Jill asks, now pacing the floor. Everyone in the room is watching her with hope in their eyes.

"Just past the main panel to the right," replies Charles. "Why?"

"Because, I've got an idea. I'm gonna need some help though." Jill is now standing in front of the man, her hands clasped onto his like talons of a hawk, her eyes silently begging him to at least hear her out.

Charles stands there a minute, Zane standing by the window gazing out into the night. It seems to have quieted outside and he thinks the snow is beautiful.

"What do we have to do?"

"Are they still out there?" Jill asks the people by the window.

"I see two of them," one person yells emphatically after everyone replies that they didn't see anything. "They're back over here walking back and forth outside the window."

"Can anybody see the third one?" After a bunch of shaking heads and responses of 'no', Jill starts to lose her composure again. "Look, people, LOOK!"

"We only see two of them," one woman insists, almost crying.

"Just great!" The nurse slams her fists against her thighs.

Charles looks at the nurse like she's crazy. "Look, I wanna help and all, but I'm not risking my ass running through a dark hospital hoping that the other generator works. That thing could be anywhere in this building."

Jill gets a devious grin on her face. "You're right, Chuck. We need a decoy"

"Don't look at me and say decoy. I'm not going. I saw what happened to Roy the Decoy." He shoves his hands into his pockets and begins to walk away.

"The morgue is down those stairs, isn't it?" asks the nurse.

Charles stops and turns to look at her, his eyebrows furrowed. "Yeah, so?"

"Let's give that thing a frozen dinner." Jill's grin has turned into a full blown smile.

"You're one sick girl, you know that?" Charles shakes his head and Zane stares at her with his eyes wider than a deer in headlights.

"Do you have a better idea? The rescue brought in two young women last night, both overdosed. We haven't had a chance to get them out of here because of the weather."

"Good, I guess."

"Good? They died and all you can say is good?" Jill snaps.

"They're already dead. We're not. That's our decoy."

Jill glares at him a second before turning to the crowd.

"Attention please. Everyone, I need to make an announcement!" She waits for everyone to quiet down before continuing. "We're gonna try and catch those things in the clinic, me and the maintenance guys."

"Wait, what?!? What do you mean 'guys'???" Zane looks like he's going to mess his pants. Jill glares at him before continuing.

"After we leave, shut off all the lights to conserve the generator. The heat will still be on and that should keep these things out." She hears a bunch of gasps and some people whispering the word 'no' "Stay out of sight and be quiet, you'll be fine. We're gonna get them to go elsewhere looking for food. They won't leave if they continue to view the main course, right?"

"Let's go," she says softly to the maintenance guys and George.

The four take off for the morgue as everyone starts to bustle about the room. Suddenly Zane pipes in. "We can get fired for going in here. The Dean of Medicine told maintenance to stay out of the morgue without permission."

"I won't tell if you won't," Jill says. "Besides, if we don't do this, you're apt to end up in the morgue anyways, only with a different view." She looks over at Charles. "Where did you get this guy, a work release program?" George laughs under his breath.

Luckily the morgue itself is in a warm section of the hospital, though inside the room is extremely cold and Jill shivers as they enter the creepiest room in the hospital.

"Does anybody know them?" she asks as they walk around the tables with the bodies on them.

"Must be from out of state," the orderly states matter-of-factly.

"Going to college probably. I've never seen them and I've lived here all my life," says Charles.

"They can't be more than 19 or 20 year old." The only woman in the group finds herself choking back tears, a lump in her throat as she begins to question her plan, wondering if she's placed this group, and the entire town, in grave danger. She's so used to being in charge she can't stop herself when it comes to trying to reach a resolution to a problem, but she realizes suddenly that she's in over her head, objectivity has blown out the window.

"What do we do with them Jill?" George walks around the table holding one girl's arm. "What a waste." He says pushing the autopsy table out of the morgue toward the elevator. He's not interested in wasting any time.

Zane follows closely behind. "I've never seen a dead body before." He jumps when the deceased girl's body slightly moves as the table rolls across the floor.

"Quit being a wuss," chides George.

Jill and Charles follow close by pushing the second body.

"Do you really think this will work?" Charles asks Jill quietly.

"I'm just hoping it gives us enough time to get to the access corridor," she whispers before speaking loudly enough for everyone to hear her. "Now remember, if you see or hear one of those things, roll one girl in its direction and run to the corridor entrance. The last one there needs to close the door tight and keep going until we're under the clinic." Jill looks around one last time. "Everyone ready?"

"As ready as we'll ever be," they respond in unison.

The group proceeds down the dark cold hallways for what feels like forever, looking everywhere around them covering each others' backs army-style as they move with the two dead bodies. They slowly advance to the corridor entrance.

"There's the door Jill!" Charles exclaims.

"I know, I see it. We're almost there." She's not ready to let out the breath she's been holding just yet.

Up ahead, down the hallway off to their left they hear a low growl. They look at each other. Jill tells George, "When we get to that corner, roll that girl's body down that hall and run for the door."

"You don't have to tell me to run. I'm gonna do my best Barry Sanders impression, EVER!"

As they get to the hallway leading left, the naked body of the dead girl being pulled is ripped off the table from behind. They start running. The naked body of the girl being pushed is ripped sideways off the second table and into the darkness. They run faster, screaming, continuously looking behind them to see if the Chillers are coming after them. The orderly is through the door first and falls to the floor. Jill runs in just behind him and turns as she holds the door for Charles and Zane.

"Run, good God," she pants, "RUN!" She screams that the Chillers are right behind them as she sees the monsters' shadows chasing the two men down the hall.

Charles gets to the door first. He turns and reaches his hand out to his assistant. "Come on Boy, we're home free." They make eye contact. Zane smiles. Suddenly his body is snatched back into the darkness by the claws of the Chillers. The maintenance super slams the door shut. He looks at Jill and the orderly.

"What the fuck was that?" He starts to frantically punch and bang on the storage lockers. "That kid's wife just had a baby girl. What's his wife gonna do now?"

Jill puts her hand on his shoulder. "We have to destroy those things and we have to do it before they kill again."

He shakes her hand off of him and glares at her in the darkness. "Shut up. This is your fault. He wouldn't have been down here if it weren't for you and your bright ideas."

George steps in and takes Charles aside. When they come back, the super apologizes to Jill.

“I’m sorry, you’re right. Let’s kill those ugly bastards.” There’s a mixture of sadness and anger in his voice.

“Where do we go?” asks Jill. She’s leaning against the wall, wringing her hands as tears roll down her cheeks.

“The light switch is over on the left wall. If we have power here it will come on.

Jill finds the switch.

Click.

Nothing.

Click Click Click.

Still nothing.

“One of these storage lockers has an extra flashlight, I’ll find it,” says Charles.

SMASH! CLANG! BANG! CLANG!

As he feels through the darkness he declares that he’s found it. The flashlight comes on. “Follow me!” he demands.

They all break into a run, Jill and George following behind him.

It takes a few minutes, but they reach their destination. “Here’s the door to the clinic’s basement.”

“Open it slowly,” Jill whispers.

He gingerly opens the door and reports the coast is clear. He flashes the light on the generator. “Pray it has fuel.” He checks and it’s only got about a twelfth of a tank.

“This isn’t gonna give us much time.” He pushes the flow lever and hits the start switch. It starts, then stalls. He repeats, and again it starts then stalls. He holds his hands as if praying then tries again. It starts a third time… and stays on.

Charles walks over to the main circuit panel and hits all the levers to “on”. He cranks the thermostat to 100 degrees. “Now what?” he asks Jill.

“We let them in.”

“We let those things in here? Are you fucking crazy? On drugs? It’s still cold in here and now they know there’s food, as in US, in here.” He points at the cellar window where the Chillers are scratching, trying to get in.

“What are those pipes for?” she asks, pointing toward the corner.

"Those are for the gas when our power is up and running. We use gas heat because it's more efficient."

"So those pipes are filled with gas?" She has an idea.

"No, only when those valves are on. When the power goes out there's a safety switch that locks out the gas. It stays in the tanks out back."

"And how do we get the gas back in the lines?"

"We'd have to manually open the valves by hand."

"Is that something you can do?"

"Yeah, I suppose I could manage it. What are you thinking, Jill?"

"Would you please just open all the valves into this building?"

"Sure, if that's really what you want. But you're just asking for trouble. One spark and we're barbecued. The safety valve isn't operational without power. This whole building could blow." Charles is concerned that Jill has lost her damn mind.

Jill nods her head up and down, almost to confirm that she is indeed off her rocker. It takes a second to register, but before long the maintenance man is also nodding with a smirk on his face.

"Ohhh…that's what we want!" He pauses a minute, while George stands back and shakes his head at the pair of them. "I think?"

"Now, get those things in here," Jill states firmly. The orderly taunts the Chillers at the window without question. The creatures don't like it.

"Those steps there, they go up to the clinic's reception area through the door. Doesn't the entrance have an automatic door opener?" asks George, becoming part of the scheming group.

"Yeah, but it doesn't work without power," Charles declares. After a brief pause he's got an idea "I could run the wire directly from the relay panel to the generator. That just might work."

"How long would that take?" asks Jill.

"Five minutes or so." He proceeds to wire the automatic door directly to the generator. The orderly continues to taunt the Chillers. They are becoming visibly agitated and aggressive. The tempered glass begins to crack as they claw at and throw themselves against it.

"Jill, those things are pissed at your friend over there. I'd appreciate it if he'd knock it off." To George he yells, "Come on, get away from those windows."

"I swear one of those things looks just like my mother-in-law."

Jill smiles and walks up the stairs to the door leading to the reception area. "Find me something I can use to hold this door open."

"Whatever!" says George. He finds a mop and hands it up to her. "Will this work?"

"I think so." She wedges it in the door's hinges. She slowly removes her hands. "Yep." It stays open.

"Good." The orderly walks back under the window. "God those things are ugly."

The maintenance super pulls out a wire and starts connecting the ends to the power relay and the generator.

"Wait!" says Jill. "Do we have any rope?"

"Yeah. In this locker." Charles nods toward the locker to his right.

Jill grabs the rope and hands it to George while Charles continues to work on the wiring. "Tie the rope to the front door and open it manually. We need to get ready to let those things in."

The RN gives the maintenance man a few more minutes to finish with the generator. "Are we ready yet?"

"Yep." Charles opens the valves to let in the gas. The goal is to get it to the disconnected hose.

"Get in the tunnel George, NOW!" Jill yells at the orderly.

"Whatever!" the orderly yells. He's watching the Chillers break out pieces of the windows trying to get in.

He walks into the dark corridor. "I can't see shit in here."

"Just feel your way through to the other end," Charles tells him. "And quit whining like a bitchy little girl."

"Damn things are probably waiting for us there."

"Do you think this will work?" asks Jill.

"We'll soon find out," says the maintenance man. "We're only gonna get one try at this."

"I know," she replies.

They walk into the dark corridor with the door held open slightly, just enough to see. She holds the rope to the door. He holds the wire to the generator.

"When I pull the wire to the connector, immediately hit the floor! The door frame is air tight but the door is lightweight. I don't know how it will do under that kind of pressure. If you have to pray, do it now!"

"I've already said my prayers," Jill responds. "I'm ready. George?" He nods. "Okay, on three."

"Okay!"

Charles pulls open the door. "Oh shit, here they come!"

"Wait…wait…THREE! Now! Pull the wire and push the fucking door shut," Jill screams.

She pulls the wire and they push the door shut and hit the dark corridor's floor.

It's quiet.

"What happened? I didn't hear anything." George picks his head up slightly.

"You missed the target. God damn it!" The nurse is pissed.

"What?" Charles is lost.

"You missed the other wire. They never touched."

Suddenly, BAM BAM! The monsters are thrusting themselves against the feeble door.

"Ohmigod, they are really pissed now. Door won't take much more of that. We have to make a run for it." George starts to stand up as the Chillers slam themselves against the glass.

"We'd never make it ten feet beyond that other door," Charles states.

"Can you sing?" asks Jill suddenly.

"Can I SING? If I could sing, do you think I'd be an orderly in this damn hospital?"

Bam, BAM!

Jill stands up and brushes herself off.

"What in the hell are you doing?" asks George.

"Decoy time." She stares at her colleague. "C'mon, sing me a song and then when I yell at you to stop, get the hell out of here." Charles continues to lie on the floor, his head swinging from George who is beside him to Jill standing over them.

"I'm not leaving this corridor. Those things are waiting for me out there." He's whining like a little bitch again.

"Okay, have it your way," Jill says. "We'll just have to do something else."

"Whatever."

"When I say the word NOW, we're gonna pull the door open. When they come in, we leave. Sound like a plan?"

"Not a very good one." Charles is piping in with his opinion.

Jill glares at both men as they start to get off the floor. "Just start running and don't look back. Now start singing, the both of you."

"I only know one song." Charles stares at his feet with embarrassment on his face, though it's not very visible in the darkness.

Jill's had enough of their whining. "FINE, whatever, just fucking sing it! The both of you are gonna drive me to drink if I ever get out of here."

"Sugar pie honey bunch, you know that I'd wait for you. I can't help myself, I love you and nobody else." Charles starts to sing and George quickly joins in when he recognizes the song.

"NOW!" Jill yells.

They open the door and Chillers enter, immediately heading toward the orderly and maintenance man. Jill slips out behind them. Charles panics and starts running for the exit. Jill stops and turns around.

GROWL

George stops singing and mutters, "Oh shit," before breaking into a run himself.

With the sounds of their running fading, Jill yells into the corridor. "I'm right here you blood sucking mutants."

All three stop chasing George and Charles and begin to advance toward her. She turns and runs as if in slow motion, like she's having a nightmare and the boogieman is after her. She gets to the steps. Looking back to the corridor she hears them coming. She jumps up the stairs 3 at a time and heads for the exit. She can see Charles out the window nearing the woods. She looks back down the steps. She sees the shadows of the Chillers on the floor. They continue to chase her. She exits the building still feeling like she's moving in slow motion as she looks back to see the Chillers closing in on her. She runs about 20 more feet and slips and falls into a mound of snow.

Just then, down the street, the crew working on the power outage has some success. "We've got power to the transformer. Hit the switch. NOW!" The electrical crew team member throws the switch at the transformer. The power source at the building sparks as power surges through the wires. This happens just as the Chillers reach the reception area of the clinic.

KABOOM!

An explosion rips through the clinic sending flames a hundred feet into the air. George watches in terror as the flames advance down the corridor directly at him. "Oh shit."

He turns and leaps out the door to the hospital hallway while flames fly over his head then disappear. He slowly gets up.

"Damn, we got lights again. Good I'm gonna call me a lawyer and sue this damn place." He wipes himself off as he heads down the hall. "I'm gonna sue somebody. Anybody. This shit is bogus."

Charles turns from where he is in the hospital yard and sees Jill dragging herself slowly on the ground, covered in pieces of sheetrock and random building materials. He runs back to assist as she slowly gets up, looking back at what was once a clinic. They look at each other and smile.

"Look, uh, about running, um, I'm sorry I left----"

"Quiet Charles, I get it. You have a couple of kids yourself, don't you? At least one, from the way you reacted when we lost Zane."

He's quiet a minute before responding. "Can I buy you a cold beer?" he asks.

"Make it a warm one and we've got a deal."

He helps her across the snow-covered yard as the others run out and give them a hand. Flames are crackling and smoke billows in layers from the building. The three Chillers lay dead in the snow. Smoke is emanating from their burnt bodies.

Jill stops walking and looks out toward the way Shotgun came in from the woods. Her mind's eye travels through the woods, retracing Shotgun's trail. Back through the town, the orchard, back down the dirt road to the warehouse. Back to the tractor trailer truck's cargo door.

BAM BAM BAM

With much more power than the now-dead Chillers had, the door is ripped to shreds. These new Chillers exit the trailer growling into the night air as they advance into the darkness. They begin running in the direction of the state's prison.

www.ingramcontent.com/pod-product-compliance
Ingram Content Group UK Ltd.
Pitfield, Milton Keynes, MK11 3LW, UK
UKHW020231250726
13967UKWH00001B/301

9 781300 026792